NONA ZUPPA

& THE PASTA PARADE

ISBN: 978-1-4834-6912-6 (sc)
ISBN: 978-1-4834-6921-8 (hc)
ISBN: 978-1-4834-6911-9 (e)

Library of Congress Control Number: 2017906807

Lulu Publishing Services rev. date: 05/10/2017

NONA ZUPPA
& THE PASTA PARADE

Written by
Gera DiSanto

Illustrated by
John Barnett

For my daughters
Giada and Giorgianna

NONA ZUPPA is the oldest living pasta maker. She makes homemade pasta and sauce every day for lunch out of her famous food truck, The Pasta Parade.

Nona Zuppa usually opens The Pasta Parade and starts her pasta making at five o'clock in the morning for the town's daily lunch.

Except for today!

NONA ZUPPA'S alarm clock didn't wake her up! She knew it must have been late when she saw the sun had begun to peep through her window.

"Oh no," Nona Zuppa cried. "It's six o'clock, and I'm an hour late!"

Nona frantically got dressed and grabbed her apron from the kitchen table on her way out the door.

AS NONA SPRINTED to the food truck, a strange feeling came over her. It was as if she knew today was going to be a mixed-up day.

When Nona finally reached the food truck, she opened the door, and to her surprise, she found all the pasta made! And all the flour and cornmeal bags she used to make it were gone.

"Baker Giuseppe, Baker Giuseppe, did you see who came into my food truck and made the pasta?"

"No, no, signora. But what a nice surprise!"

Nona wondered, *Could there be pasta-making elves living in her truck?*

"I better start preparing the pasta and sauces for lunch before it gets really late."

When lunch was over, Nona Zuppa cleaned up the food truck and headed home.

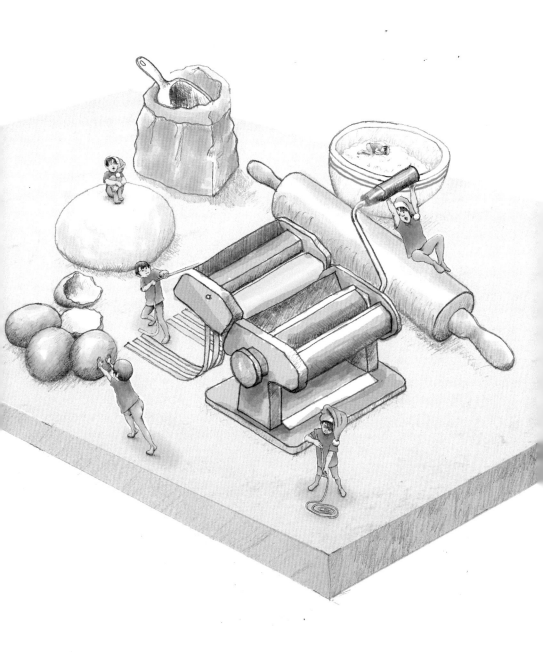

THE NEXT MORNING, Nona Zuppa was glad to wake up on time. On the way to the food truck, a funny feeling came over her just as it had the day before.

When Nona arrived at the food truck, she was upset. Baker Giuseppe hadn't dropped off the bags of flour and cornmeal she needed to make the pasta. Lunch was going to be late!

Nona Zuppa quickly opened the door to the food truck. Inside, she found all the pasta out on the counter, drying. It was as if she had discovered a treasure chest of homemade pasta!

"Baker Giuseppe, Baker Giuseppe, do you know who made the pasta today?"

"No, no, signora," Baker
Giuseppe replied.

AS NONA ZUPPA prepared the sauces, her granddaughters, Gigi and Giorgi, came to visit. "Hi, Nona," they sang.

"Hi, girls," Nona answered.

"Nona, it's very busy today. May we help you! Please, Nona, please, may we help?" they cried.

"Girls, it's really busy, and I can't have you back here getting in the way."

"We won't. We promise."

"Okay, okay. But please don't make a mess!" Nona Zuppa cried. "You both can bag the food orders. But don't get in the way, please!"

Gigi and Giorgi put the pasta containers in the take-out bags. Nona Zuppa was delighted to have some help.

"**N**ONA, DON'T YOU LIKE having help?" Gigi asked.

"Yes, I do! And thank you, girls, for not making a mess."

"We never make a mess," replied Giorgi. "I've been so good at making the pasta. I didn't even spill any flour on the floor when I poured it into the mixer."

"Giorgi," grunted Gigi.

"What are you talking about?" asked Nona.

"Giorgi, you can never keep a secret!"

"What? We need to tell Nona Zuppa our surprise," said Giorgi.

"A surprise!" Nona gasped.

"Nona, we've been making the pasta before you get to work in the morning. Giorgi and I asked Baker Giuseppe if he could let us in when he delivered the flour and cornmeal. We've seen how tired you are at the end of each day, and we thought it would be a good idea to help you."

NONA WAS SO HAPPY to discover her granddaughters were helping to make the pasta. "Thank you, girls. I'm so grateful for all of your help. Would you like to come and help Nona every day?"

Gigi and Giorgi were so excited to work with Nona during summer vacation.

"Yes, yes, we'll make the pasta every day and bag the lunches. Just like we did today!" Gigi shouted.

The next morning, Gigi and Girogi were bursting with energy. They ran to the food truck to help Nona make the pasta.

NONA'S FAVORITE PASTA RECIPE

Recipe

2 cups of flour
3 eggs
pasta maker

On a clean surface (countertop or cutting board), create a mountain with the flour. Make a small well in the flour just big enough to hold the eggs.

In a bowl, lightly beat the eggs. Add to the flour, and using your hands, mix the eggs and flour until you have a ball of dough. Continue to knead the dough so all the flour and egg is mixed together.

Sprinkle a little more flour onto the surface, and roll out the dough into a thin pancake or sheet.

Take the sheet of dough and place it through the slot of a crank-style pasta maker with your favorite pasta shape and crank through the machine. If using an electric pasta maker, follow the machine's instructions.

Photo courtesy of Olivia Wilcox

GERA DISANTO has been in the education field as a teacher for over fifteen years. As a mother of two young girls, she always found herself entertaining for special occasions. Her extensive knowledge of food came from her childhood growing up in the family restaurant. She lives with her family in Rhode Island.

Recipe

Recipe

Recipe

Recipe